ex libris

by

Max Ehrmann

photographs by

Marc Tauss

scholastic press   new york

Desiderata

words for life

Desiderata: words for life copyright © 2003 by Scholastic Press
Photographs copyright © 2003 by Marc Tauss
ISBN 0-439-67368-2
The Library of Congress has cataloged the jacketed hardcover edition as follows:
Ehrmann, Max, 1872-1945.
Desiderata: words for life / by Max Ehrmann;
photographs by Marc Tauss.— 1st ed.   p. cm.
Summary: Presents the text of the well-known inspirational poem that
advises one to "go placidly amid the noise and haste" because "you are a
child of the universe, no less than the trees and the stars."
ISBN 0-439-37293-3
1. Conduct of life—Juvenile poetry. 2. Children's poetry, American.
[1. Conduct of life—Poetry. 2. American poetry.] I. Tauss, Marc, ill.
II. Title.   PS3509.H7   D38 2003   811'.52—dc21 2002004733
10 9 8 7 6 5 4 3 2   04 05 06 07
Printed in Singapore 46
The photographs in this book were shot with large
format, medium format, and handmade cameras.
The text type was set in Venetian 301 BT.
Art direction and design by Marijka Kostiw

IN CELEBRATION OF TWO PEOPLE WHO WENT "PLACIDLY AMID THE NOISE AND HASTE" AND DEDICATED THEIR LIVES TO MAKING
A DIFFERENCE IN THE WORLD, A TOTAL OF 2% OF THE SUGGESTED RETAIL PRICE OF EVERY BOOK SOLD WILL GO TO CHILDREN'S
INTERNATIONAL SUMMER VILLAGES, FOUNDED BY DR. DORIS T. ALLEN, AND TO THE DANIEL PEARL FOUNDATION, INDEPENDENT,
NONPROFIT, NONPOLITICAL ORGANIZATIONS THAT SEEK TO FOSTER PEACE THROUGH CROSS-CULTURAL UNDERSTANDING. TO
FIND OUT MORE ABOUT THESE ORGANIZATIONS VISIT THEIR WEB SITES AT WWW.CISVUSA.ORG AND WWW.DANIELPEARL.ORG.
THE PURCHASE OF THIS BOOK IS NOT TAX DEDUCTIBLE.

In loving memory of my

Aunt Birdie's laughter

— M. T.

Go placidly

amid the noise and haste,

and remember what peace

there may be in silence.

As far as possible without surrender

be on

good terms

with all persons.

Speak your truth

quietly and clearly; and listen to others,

even to the dull and the ignorant; they too have their story.

Avoid loud and aggressive persons,

they are vexatious to the spirit.

If you compare yourself with others,

you may become vain or bitter,

for always

there will be greater

and lesser persons

than yourself.

Enjoy

your achievements

as well

as your plans.

Keep interested

in your own career, however humble;

it is a real possession in the changing fortunes of time.

Exercise caution in your business affairs;

for the world is full of trickery.

But let this not blind you to what virtue there is;

many persons strive for

high ideals,

and

everywhere

life is full

of

heroism.

Be yourself.

Especially do not feign affection.

Neither be cynical

about love; for in the face of all aridity and disenchantment

it is as perennial as the grass.

Take kindly the counsel of the years,

gracefully surrendering the things of youth.

Nurture strength

of spirit to shield you in sudden misfortune.

But do not distress yourself with dark imaginings.

Many fears are born of fatigue and loneliness.

Beyond

a wholesome

discipline,

be

gentle

with yourself.

You
are
a child
of the
universe,

no less than the trees and the stars;

you have a right to be here.

And whether or not it is clear to you,

no doubt

the universe

is unfolding

as it should.

Therefore

be at peace

with God, whatever you conceive Him to be.

And whatever your labors and aspirations,

in the noisy confusion of life,

keep peace in your soul.

With all its sham, drudgery

and broken dreams,

it is still a

beautiful world.

Be cheerful.

Strive to be happy.

ABOUT "DESIDERATA"

Max Ehrmann wrote his most famous poem, "Desiderata," in 1927, while living in his hometown of Terre Haute, Indiana. He shared it with friends as part of a Christmas greeting in 1933. Sometime thereafter, a Boston psychiatrist discovered the poem. When he was on active duty with the U.S. Army in the South Pacific during World War II, he wrote to Ehrmann, "I think you should know that nearly every day of my life I use your very fine prose poem 'Desiderata' in my work." He also obtained Ehrmann's permission to distribute copies of "Desiderata" to the soldiers.

In 1948, three years after his death, Ehrmann's widow had "Desiderata," along with other works, published in *The Poems of Max Ehrmann*, edited by Bertha K. Ehrmann. In the 1950s, a Maryland pastor copied "Desiderata" onto the front page of a small booklet of inspirational writings he had put together for his congregation. It was printed on the church letterhead, which read: "Old St. Paul's Church, Baltimore, A.D. 1692." From there, the poem must have passed from hand to hand, and along the way, the founding date of the church, 1692, was confused for the copyright date of the poem. "Desiderata" was falsely believed to be age-old wisdom preserved from an anonymous author.

Soon after, the poem gained enormous popularity, albeit without proper accreditation. It was reprinted in books, on posters, and on cards throughout the world; recorded as a narrative song; and became a mantra during the sixties "peace and love" movement. Perhaps it even fulfilled Max Ehrmann's own wish, which he wrote in his diary in 1921: "I should like, if I could, to leave a humble gift—a bit of chaste prose that had caught up some noble moods. . . ."

Certainly "Desiderata" secures for Max Ehrmann a place among the canon of visionary writers who have bestowed the gift of revealing a simple, enduring truth with clarity and grace.

Max Ehrmann was born in 1872 in Terre Haute, Indiana, to German immigrant parents. He graduated from DePauw University and went on to study philosophy and law at Harvard. He is the author of more than twenty books, including poetry, plays, short stories, essays, and novels.

Max Ehrmann died in 1945.

Marc Tauss's intriguing photographs have graced countless book jackets. His first picture book, *Leaf by Leaf: Autumn Poems* selected by Barbara Rogasky, was published to starred reviews, including *School Library Journal's* rave, "Tauss's ethereal color and black-and-white photographs capture the imagery of the verse and extend past the boundaries of the page. . . . A bountiful feast."

Marc Tauss lives in New York City.